BRAiN EXPLOSiON

A COLLECTION OF THOUGHTS, VERBIAGE, ASSORTED QUOTABLES AND PROFUNDITIES

by DAVE SHELTON

Former *National Lampoon* Senior Writer and Head of Cartoons

BearManor Media

2013

Brain Explosion: A Collection of Thoughts, Verbiage,
Assorted Quotables and Profundities

© 2013 Dave Shelton

For information, address:

BearManor Media
P. O. Box 71426
Albany, GA 31708

bearmanormedia.com

Published in the USA by BearManor Media

ISBN— 1-59393-267-7
978-1-59393-267-1

"I like watching creativity play out. Dave Shelton possesses an imagination that balances darkness and innocence in a very insightful array of cartoons, conversations and musings. It's the work of a free mind, and a template like that has a value all its own, particularly these days. Sweet and sardonic, it's good stuff."

– Rick Overton (Emmy® winning actor/writer)

"What is the best and worst I can say about Dave Shelton's talents? The best is he is innovative, creative, funny, and brilliant. The worst is he does not have the ability to clone himself."

– Stephen Furst (Award winning Producer/actor)

"I'm proud to be Dave's friend. I'm proud of his book. You will see and sense this wonderful talent to amuse all."

– Kevin Dobson (Emmy® nominated actor/director)

"Out of the mouths of babes... Well, even though Dave Shelton may not be a babe, his musings and observational wit are sure to click with many. Sharp and very much on point, he shows you our world through his art and unique perspective."

– Charlie Chiodo (Emmy® nominated producer/visual FX producer)

"Adorably Bizarre; Originally Eclectic; Creatively Scattered"

"How could you not fall in love with Dave Shelton's thoroughfare of Genius?"

– Dana Barron (Emmy® award winning actress, Mother and Philanthropist)

"Fun, witty and full of surprise, Dave Shelton delivers a much needed antidote to today's stressful lives. Grab this book during the day to enjoy a few pages or sit down with it for a longer time: feel anxiety slip away and the giggles set in. Dave delivers the laughter that we all yearn for and that is in such short supply today. Get Brain Explosion and your own mind will explode with mirth, madness, and merriment. Kudos to my friend, Dave."

– Kathy Garver (Halo and Audie Award winning iconic TV actress)

"When Dave Shelton was a youngster, he was cognizant of his talent as an artist and writer. Now that he is a young adult, he has proven it professionally. As a result, he is now being admired and respected by an appreciative public for his contribution to the arts. Read this book and enjoy."

– June Foray (legendary voice actress)

Dedicated To:

Tami Zorge, my funny sweet slob, my love, my inspiration, my greatest ass-et.

ACKNOWLEDGEMENTS

Special Thanks

Agnes May
Brandi Hackitt
Brian Ceponis
Cary Kozlov
Charlie Chiodo
Dana Barron
Danielle Spencer
Eric Chamberlain
Grammy
James Dinteman
Joy Harmon
June Foray
Kathy Garver
Kevin Dobson
Kevin Grant
Martin Klebba
Mckenzie Rice
Rick Overton
Robbin Cafagna
Robert Richards
Ron Soffer
Stephen Furst
Zachary Alexander Rice

My family

Everyone who ever believed in me and those who didn't
(which made me even more determined)

Introduction

And so it begins...

As a writer and cartoonist, I am constantly looking for sources of inspiration, perspiration and just plain ideas that don't suck. With the onset of the internet, social media, and a constant bombardment of electronic and virtual stimuli it is not difficult to find those sources of information. Yet, on the other hand, all of it could also be a complete waste of input and a total immersion into a cesspool of literary crapulence.

With that, and the fact that I can't turn my brain off for any longer than it takes a dust bunny to form a litter on my linoleum floor, I turned on my cerebral faucet and let the liquid verbiage flow free and what came out can either incite, infuriate, repulse or inspire. In any case, and in my never ending dealings with modern society on their way to complete mental annihilation, I present this collection in no particular order... of course with love.

Dave Shelton

And so it still begins….

I asked a girl out to dinner because she said she was already out to lunch.

Don't go looking for a soul mate with someone without a soul.

Obscurity sucks.

You're out of this world. Do you get a return ticket?

You can sit in a puddle of your own pity, but don't rain on my parade.

Isn't it amazing how most people with high IQs can be so stupid?

New rock group: Spew and the Phlegmtones.

The Beast that Ate My F*&@#n' Penis: a new movie starring Andrew Dice Clay.

Scary moments: When the toilet is flushed and instead of whirlpooling down, it rises to the edge of the bowl and you just know it is going to tidal over the edge in one big gush of sewage. There is nothing scarier than a stuffed toilet.

Two ways to wear a dress in Hollywood; tight or off.

Q: What did the hypochondriac writer say to the doctor?
A: I'm working on my new book doc about things I say and I am featuring all my aneurysms.

I'd like to take condemned people, tear them down, and put up sex toys in their place.
Smokers are like old 8-track cassettes. They interrupt right in the middle of a conversation and are part of a trend that died off.

The mall is a place young people go to buy friends.

The ability of people to express themselves without using profanity is gone. Isn't it an f*&$#n' shame?

Later in the peace mode.

If someone gives you their helping hand only after you've made it, give them a helping finger.

Selective Prudality: The disdain for one form of sexuality while being OK about others. Eg: It's alright to practice free love when you're participating in it, but not when you have to watch 2 elderly people doing it.

Smugness and Arrogance are often just covers for inadequacy.

Why do people have to die? It's God's way of letting people know how they lived.

Soul Colonic: cleansing bad energy.

Pay to Pay existence: living to pay bills.

If you had a small penis how would you feel? I wouldn't.

I'm going to form a band...what are you going to do in it?...back-up vocals....how far back?

My brain is so fried nothing is coming to mind.

All you talk about is stuff.

I live in a delusion of happy moods.

I was born a child unbeknownst to myself.

You're a fun girl...and you're a fungi.

Where did you hear that? I heard about it in my mind.

Even when I'm hurting, my brain works.

Word: Snice: sweetly nice.

Don't forget to wipe the snob off your nose.
Excuse me, but I believe you have some snob on your nose.

I'll talk, you lift (gabby friends you ask to help move).

You follow absurdity a little too closely.

You shouldn't think with your mouth full.

I've never seen a day actually break.

FLEA TRAP:

Movie Names: *Weird House, The Willies, Turbotoids, Terror Reid*

He was so boring, when he talked, even his foot fell asleep.

Character: The Paisley Knight (colorful costumes, deceiving, can beat the Black Hood)

The way things are going in our world, you can either be a solution or the result and we're running out of results.

If you can't come in first, come in handy.

Their earnings were so small he took out a second mortgage on his tent.

Band name...Delusions of Psycho...Dannie Smackcheese and the Isolated Incidents

If you can't get paid, at least make it pay off.

He should spend more time on preparation and less on celebration.

You start the road to stardom with looks and reach it with talent.

I have so much mouthwash and oral rinse in me, I'm a walking disinfectant.

He's a deep thinker in a shallow pool.

Don't get jugular on me, I like when that dog went jugular on him.

Title: False promises from the litho world.

I know someone so obsessive compulsive he could give the sidewalk a neurosis.

You keep the light on in my soul.

Character Idea: Random Guy – when you need no one in particular with no particular powers (inspired by Adriana Patti).

I'm so far swimming in debt, I have to wear a bathing suit just to look at my credit card statements.

Film Idea: Change the Channel – A remote causes TV shows to come to life for real.

TITLE: *Death of the Snot-ball Ring*

People who make others feel guilty better have a good karma attorney.

People who hurt others should look up a lot…you never know when karma will fall.

Hi, I'm the new nerd in town. Do you have any kids my brain level to play with?

NAMES: Genius Thinkman, I.Q. Genius, Miles Long

The sheep police will make you sweat-er.

You just tripped over an imaginary plane of existence.

Gag me with sentiment.

He has no assets, so if I sue him, the only things I can get are the first three letters of the word asset, and no way do I want any piece of that ass.

Song: *CAT AND LOVE*

> Oh frustration
> the tail of the cat
> that cuts through like daggers to the heart
> and hell's fury
> the fury that bites to the soul
> and scars where once a feline lept
> cats and love
> so as symbiotic might they be
> can empty be more
> than a casual brush with a memory
> and cats and love will reign
> for as their fate allows
> their destinies are kept like purrs
> or what difference does it make
> that cats and love are going
> and what is left is dark
> and realms of dirty dogs shall scavenge
> the scapes of cats and love
> and leave them too soon a thought
> while pity feeds on cats and love the rest of eternity

Names: The Pasta Bros, Caveman Academy

How could you read in the dark? I went to night school.

Are you a complete idiot, or is your development not complete yet?

A young kid disillusioned with school bathrooms with no stall doors: "How's a kid supposed to give a crap anymore?!"

She is self into herself.

Everybody wants to be a maverick, but no one wants to ride the horse.

Song: *FRESH SISTER*

Jack your load all down my mind
leave your world so far behind
I've gone off to a better place
there they have no human race
where there's no such thing as hate
or condemned to some master's fate
'cause you can't get yourself a date
resolved to that bitter waste
fresh sister
down on your knees
you are begging to pagaen disease
fresh sister
when it's over seek the soil delight
then your sun is by pale moonlight
I have got no patience divine
let your fingers linger crossing the line
yeah, I said to jack your load so
did you think I would conform to your rules no
I am the past reincarnate
I am the lost possessions of all that's been buried
but when the sun burns the point till your skin dissolves
and your skeleton falls
I will be the only bond to reinvent your soul

Do talkative people who live in their cars wake up with motor mouth?

Song: *CUT*

>   open up your eyes and see
>   what the world was meant to be
>   there's a sun that's shining bright
>   let us walk into the light
>   cut your worries down to size
>   cut your worries down to size
>   cut your worries down
>   and leave them linger far behind
>   when you're down it's such a drag
>   making me feel just as bad
>   take a look and you will see
>   euphoric pleasure just like me

Terms: Momular, Lamo in a box, Buster Crabb's crabs, I give that the scam sign, pitching a frog, Miss Interpret, her pet bird Squawks A. Lott, Masterbation Theater.

Life is a gas and we are all the cars.

In the urban jungle, you make blood angels in the concrete.

Line: Rhinestone devils on the outskirts of town

Adult book title: *Gift of the Vagi*

Book title: *Donuts Are Free*, the story of a liberated chocolate and creme eclair as he glazes a trail of icing across the west

Book title: *This Property is Condamned*

You need to get into the chill zone

Common law is defined as it is common that you better be happy with whatever you get.

You know you're a dating pariah when girls start texting each other the same excuse to cancel dates and your mother gave it to them.

May he rest in peace who's never been born

VILLIAN name: Vector Mortic

If you don't hear a dog in the forest do you think it could be barking up the wrong tree?

Band names: Druid and the Renderers, Soul Scream Fudge.

You've scratched your last piece of humanity.

NAMES: Betty Luksatcox, Gerta Grip, Prude Danish, Lester Letch (or Lux) and the Sick Boys, Chad Flitt., Sir Wanksalot, Granny Sacs.

Band names: Lust Package, The Gerbel Conspiracy.

Tongue Twisters: Tartared teeth taste tainted tender teets…
painted paul puts peaceful pets on pearled people in public…
gesturing joanne jumps gingerly jacking jill in jelly…. .

Title: *Henry's Horror House*

Getting in the circle of things (in the know).

A good name for a pill popper: Perky Dan

A guy to his girlfriend who just made him spaghetti: "I love the
way you soften my noodle, sweetie."

Song: *AND THE SILENCE*

> I close my eyes and I go to my place
> where memories haven't been made
> and my dreams are still yet of endless possibilities
> and time is my field of thought where I am the key
> oh, what thoughts and passions and sweet smells are there
> and the silence, amorous red silence
> and the serenity of snow laden country lanes
> surrounded by the beauty of my fantasies
> and the images and relics of traditions and family
> you got a long train, you got a long mile, you got a long
>   time to wait
> before your work is done, before you go in style listen to me
> what did you accomplish son, why did it take so long
> what did you finish with
> that says to me it's really worth it
> that says to me hey, it's for you and not for me old man.

Well sweetie, three coins in the fountain don't make a bank account.

Life is a circus, and we are all the clowns.

You are my moosh nana.

Name: N. Trusiv.

Have you heard of that old Dicken's tale, *David Coppafeel*?

Just 'cause guys have dicks doesn't make them hard.

Joke: Two spricters and a latterator walk into a bar. One says to the bartender, "You speak with dangling participles." A casual imbiber at the bar responds, "No he doesn't. He doesn't even let them in the bar."

Are you wearing white for purity? Then you should be wearing off white.

Girl: I'm better at catching than throwing.
Guy: Yeah, I'll bet you caught every guy you threw a pass at.

Do you know what you are talking about?
I'm a rich, preppy snot, I don't have to know what I'm talking about.

Did you know that cows have two stomachs? Yeah, one and the udder one.

Man to stuck-up person: "No, really? Tell me again. It'll give me a chance to see your mouth move.

Truism: Cows wag their tails as an aeration system for their cow farts.

New shows... Television for picnic goers- the unknown entity.

Tirade: "You know, I was fine 'til you got all tiradically rexed about it.

If I feed you a suggestion, do you suppose you can digest it or would you need to ingest the whole idea?

I could see you but I was asleep. But I knew you were watching me. I could see you in your dreams.

You have to pay for this and that. Well I have this, and who needs that.

Rock group: Kaye Whie and the Festive Textures (singing their hit song "It takes a bitchin' woman to make a cheatin' man").

Country band: The Hershey Syrup Boys and The Chocolate Milk Band.

People are so quick to judge someone else, even by association. If someone has a relative, or friend, or spouse who has done something not socially or politically acceptable, then by association, that someone should be the same way or capable of the same actions or traits. Well, that is bull. People react this way because they are probably that way already and go into denial by putting the blame on someone else to steer attention away from them. It is OK for them to have these characteristics, but no, not to be exhibited by others, especially those in the public eye. This is a paradox and an oxymoron of the most disgusting proportions.

Super heroes: Innuendo Man and Biting Humor Boy.

The Deaderly Hillbillies theme song: "Yeah, that's black urine, Missouri phlegm. Well the first thing you know, old Bill's a walking corpse. Gangreen pox first did away his horse. The GOP's said we'll bury you at sea. It's safer there to decontaminate disease."

I knew a woman who was so spoiled, if you take her out of the fridge, she'd rot.

A mime may be a terrible thing to waste, but you can ignore it 'til it goes away.
What's yours is mime.

We make as much sense together as eating chocolate cake with a diet soda.

A confused woman: "I wanted to marry a guy just like my mother."

Expression: I just want to turn that frown into a clown… in other words, cheer up, bozo!

Why go through life as a pebble when you can ROCK.

I'll have you know, I can get anyone I please… that's pretty hard to do when you don't please anyone.

People think of me as quite a prize… yeah, consolation prize.

Don't you have anything better to do than pick on me?… yeah, but I didn't want you to feel neglected.

Well, I never… the way you look, I'm not surprised.

Why don't you pick on someone your own size?… 'cause I'm tired of beating up on myself.

What kind of idiot do you think I am?… I don't know, what kinds are there?

If I had a dime for every time I came up with a bright idea, I still couldn't afford the bulb.

I don't have to stay here and listen to your insults… why, where do you usually go?

Why are you such an obvious moron?… 'cause I don't like to hide my feelings.

Does your mother know how ugly you are?… she should, when I was born, the doctor asked "paper or plastic?"

Contributory: adding support or responsibility to something some people might say to totally embarrass their asses.

Names: Jimmy Stilsmall, a midget. Ivan Analitch.

I do have a sense of humor… it's just hidden under this incredible wit.

She's got slim integrity (just a little bit of it).

I didn't want you to have soiled breasts so I washed your bras.

You're my little hunions.

She's history, you're a current event.

They call him…little tripod.

I have a G-rated mind in an R-rated body.

Today's weather is tepid with partial dullness and a strong chance of sports bottle.

Stupid idea: A werewolf field trip to Silver Springs.

I don't want to get drunk on regular Budweiser. Instead I want a Buzz light.

Alternative to the Ivy League… the Poison Ivy League.

I just saw Freda Payne and her brother Rectal. She sang her big hit dedicated to him, "Band of Goldbond."

You may be just in time, but we came too soon and now it's way too late.

Grampire: an old vampire.

INSECURE PERSONNEL DIRECTOR......

I need an upper class dinner at a middle class price.

This show definitely needs television adhesive.

I'm hyperextenuating (stretching really far for an excuse or alibi).

Dreams are dormant realities waiting for a wake-up call.
Nightmares are dreams we do not wish to wake up. And,
Deja Vu is reality's repeat of a daydream.

The gap in your teeth is something God gave you, not gingivitis.

I can't do things like getting work done because we have a waste
of time policy here.

Product idea: dry cleaned tampons.

Product: Color Blinders: sunglasses designed to block out
racism.

I've never heard your mouth go so deep into the dirt.

The desk is so messy it's become the Bermuda desk-triangle.

Superstition comes from all different directions but good.

I come from nowhere but myself.

Stop yelling at my throat.

Disgusting things only gross me out when I have to look at
them.

Words: Sugar Puss-wimp, Weirdnodes.

Provacilate: supporting a cause because of peer or popular belief, often proven wrong.

Googlinate: to google, to cause to go insane.

Poxity: a sickened feeling, repulsion.
Blottage carpal: bone in the blottage region of the pancreas.
Shitelings: British liars.
Susie Cream Cheese: the perfect little sweetie, to the point of maudlin.
Bostaric: overdone, overacted obsequious behavior.
Invalidic: pertaining to being bed or wheel chair ridden.
The Clown Escape: an unsuccessful bust out from jail, school, etc.
Intracated: involved with or in as in a scandalous situation.
Blibberish: nonsense.
Professorial Doctorations: junk teachers tell you that pass for education, does not include the important stuff teachers tell you.
Textations: sent texts meant to keep you texting.

When you go to the movies, do you ever wonder if you are making the movie up as you watch?

Rock group name: Canned Peaches.

LIFE IS:
• Going out with someone less fortunate just to make you look bigger, and then finding out that they're doing the same thing.
• Making a really annoying noise at the movies just to be obnoxious and then finding out the audience consists entirely of deaf people.
• Driving in your car and you hear a great joke on the radio and at the punch line you drive under a bridge and lose the signal.
• Having a piece of food on your face, not noticing, and wondering why no one will look at you.

- Having someone kiss up to you because they think you're a big producer and, when they find out you're not, they totally ignore you.
- Having someone treat you like crap and then when they find out you're a big producer treat you like royalty. Life is then telling them to f… off.

A Dream:
On a kitchen table are welfare statements and food stamps. A pathetic looking guy in his 40s, unshaven, pudgy, wearing a stained tank undershirt and light brown khaki pants and white socks is sitting at the table. The kitchen is filthy, dirty dishes in the sink, tattered curtains blowing casually from the breeze coming in from the window over the kitchen sink. A train whistle in the distance doesn't stir any reaction from the eerily quiet man. A fly lands on his forehead. Sweat begins to bead. The fly and his forehead become animated cartoons. The fly walks across his forehead. Then the scene moves past the fly and zooms into the man's head fading into a vortex of black and enters into an antique wooden toy chest where the man is dancing like a music box ballerina. Then his head turns into a fly head, and then a zombie and a woman in a little girl's party dress appear. An image of the man's eye appears over the scene like a transparency and when two hands pull apart the eye's pupil, and a greenish yellow fluid begins to pour out onto the man and the zombie and dancer, I wake up.

Life is a bizarre series of occurrences.

Nightie Nites: well dressed sleep walkers about town.

Phrases:
Productive waste.
Lacid visualizations.
Hurl Girl.

Absence makes the heart go pitter patter.

I called you because I wanted to talk to nobody.

The world is a butterball and we're all little turkeys.

Tongue Buster: fiery fingers were flying furiously.

I ripped up my intentions.

Penny, a waitress, replied to the question, "Do you have any diet soda?" with "No, but we do have diet coke."

I think I'll move to Kansas and open a Toto farm.

The only thing Dr. McCoy fights with is boredom… and he frequently loses.

She's suffering from Dermus Notticus.

I used to have a hair lip but thanks to Pat I can now talk out of both sides of my mouth.

Industry this!!!

Rock group: Pig's Revenge, Smashed Mushies.

I really heard someone say this: "I didn't know 7:30 came twice in one day."

I can smell the air of wealth and I want to breathe.

If you have to get stoned you might as well rock.

If you can't be a billionaire, at least be a millionaire. Anything is better than being a povertaire.

Poetry:
Read me to forever sleep… 'oer never let me die… without the know that you are her, my breath beckons heaven's door to open I would be but a torn page and my life would be an unfinished journey through an unauthorized novel.

"I've lost track of time because I've been too busy."
"Yeah, I've lost track 'cause I want to be busy."

I've been dragged across the arid plains of disguised intentions.

I'm dripping with creamsicle.

You're entitled to your opinion as long as you keep it yourself.

Observation: Stars aren't unapproachable, they're just marketed that way.

I don't want to live in the wilderness. I would rather live in the vicinity of consumer products.

I'm easily pleased. I get excited over toilet paper on the roll.

Someone took oblivious and turned it to the left.

Poet thoughts:
The wind-you are an angel sent to me by the wind.
I saw you once inside a thought.
Only in words can the heart be heard, only in song can the words take flight. There is nothing so sweet as a sonnet meant to take us to places far away.
Where is the place I've dreamt of that the likes of me can go? It couldn't be just any old place, it'd have to have room for you. It has to be a place my heart has made available every single day, the kind of world we could run to, an exclusive hide-a-way.
We could greet our guests at the end of the walk, at the gate of our little white picket fence. We would spare no small expense, you would be our welcome friends.
This is how you see me, this is what you get, this wreck you see before you hasn't developed quite as yet.

Sometimes, arrogance is good. It's the only thing I have to survive. When people get me down in every urban town, it's not a bad thing. You've given me the talent, you've given me the ability, now give me the opportunity, it's a true sense of thought.

Projected Frustration: The freeway is backed up… the whole world is backed up.

I'm playing with polka dot submarines in happyland.

You're why love exists.

Beauty doesn't run in your family because you already caught it.

She's a peach in a bucket of pears and a flower in a field of weeds.

No one wants to be the boss of empty pockets.

Bumper sticker for an electric car: If you can read this, push me.

I had a friend who had a son because he always wanted a big brother.

You're my lost soul liquidator because you clear out my "where"-house.

You were my rental but I took out an option to buy.

Welcome to siren central.

I'm gonna start a town called 'Melt City' and you will be the first Mayor.

When you smile the whole world lights up. When you're sad, the whole world floods.

It was a spongie little quicky (short shower).

If I have to live in reality, I'm going to live in a reality with a dream world attached.

If you were a newspaper article you'd be on the front page and you'd be good news.

It's better to be a cool good actor than just a good actor. Put two actors of the same caliber in the same part and I guarantee the more popular personality will have a bigger audience. It's clear and proven over and over. Audiences go to see an actor not just for their acting but for their personality.

Title: Mr. Opus' Holiday Spa.

Character: Bi-functional Hamster

You're the reason we have life before we go to heaven.

Title: Developmental Interventionist.

New word: Giantacular (you're a very awesome large person).

Names: Fannie Fullovsores, Farnum Rumproast, Miles Long, Marvin Papercut, Jerry Ripshispantz, Jerry Getsithard, Richard Undergrowth, Leslie Imaman, Leslie Likesumhard, Patrick Longsucker, Perry Poopman, John Portopotte, Dick Spittlecup, Harry Pitts, Anesto Hardcox, Johnnie Wantstadie, Barnie Stukinshitz, Paul Baerer, Jake Jerkmioff, Ginger Vitis, Gerry Atrix, Phil M. Upp, Joanne Doesantcare, Les Biggerinlife, Dave Makesumkum, Joanne Licksumdrie, Joanne Luvsalez, Harry Balsuvrock, Hardlee Everfux, Connie Scareduvquakes, Marshall Criesalotz, Angeline Bamherbuns, Pat Luvsadike, Herschel Luvslox, Julia Sitsatop, Wanda Whyursmall, Hetta Longball.

You're my sunny sigh.

You're my sweet slob.

Slogan for world peace: Be nice to your neighbor. It will make a world of difference.

A negative is just a positive on the wrong line.

Little things that help other people are not so little in results.

I found my magic when I found you.

This sunset is like someone's soul burst open on the horizon.

Awful Super-Hero: Clipboard Man. He runs the loading dock at an Office Supply store. His power is being able to inventory supplies for Clark Kent.

There's nothing near Uranus but your assteroid belt.

You're so stuck up that when you sit down you sit on your pomp-ass.

What do you call a field with an attitude? Pamp-ass grass (thank you Tami).

If you plan on having sex with an old man the only sex toy you might want to consider is a defibrillator.

We're connected at the soul.

I said it in my head, not from my mouth.

Q: What do you get when you mix a kidney bean with a swimming pool?
A: A backyard in Florida

Q: Why didn't the dad pick up his kid from the baseball game?
A: 'Cause the kid said he just ran home.

The reason why handicaps Aren't the great equalizers.

On the edge of chunky (borderline fat).

Alabaster slob.

Unsolicited behavior pattern.

Without brakes, how can we stop the flood of ignorance?

It was so windy, people were flying off the handle.

"What time do you have to get up in the morning?" "I'll know when I wake up." "I'll know by morning."

Film name: Dead and Breakfast.

I even like hearing you breathe.

When you look in the mirror, there you are.

Opinions are like assholes, everyone has one and no one likes to look at them.

Let's all play in the flower field.

Title: The Moron Chronicles.

I reined her in with practicality.

Have you ever had so much love thrown at you?

Love is looking at you and seeing your soul through the reflections in your eyes.

He's not the brightest reflection in the puddle.

We're playing 'Winter' rules, right?

The rules say you have to play it there.

Delivering a speech.

Eat my dust.

Getting the upper hand.

Hauling Ass.

Seeing the world in a new light.

Name: Grubby McBuck.

I don't live on Mt. Rush Me you know. Slow down.

I'll call you when I'm back to abnormal.

There once was a stupid sex maniac without a sense of lick.

Expressions: Late O'clock. Early O'clock.

It's a long road, I'm glad I brought extra shoes.

I'm so clumsy, I tripped over a suggestion.

It's written all over my angst.

Mind over fatter.

Cool business.

Modular Perception.

They're not slow, their brains are just still in park.

A smiling stranger doesn't mean they're crazy, they just notice your limited thinking.

I'm an eternal Hopetimist.

If I can't send it through the mail, I'll send it emailically.

I look at things not just half-filled, I look at them full-filled.

Walk with trust, not stupidity.

Scouring the world.

**Who cares what it looks like? I didn't take this class
'cause I can paint.**

Elvis was so fat he *couldn't* leave the building.

**Dr. Livingwelle discovers evidence that the first cave people
may not have been as primitive as once thought.**

Early Roman entertainment executives.

Freudian Slip.

**Mac Faxtor revolutionizes movie make-up with his
mis-use of charcoal based cosmetics.**

Emil Bagela invents the first edible wheel.

Town name: Frustration, Wyoming.

Latitude improvement.

Fool me once, my problem. Fool me twice, big problem.

If the people at the bottom looked to the sides instead of up, they'd see more people that way, and would notice that it's not so lonely at the bottom.

I never make the same mistake twice, I just move on to another one.

SONG: (for Kathy Elizabeth Murphy) Party girl, just one more beer & the check's in the mail… party girl, party girl, down the road I've got the tickets to hell, to hell, to hell…I see the ranger man, he says no stop sign, I see a stranger there, he's lost his mind, party, party, party girl.

Q: What did the router say to the computer who asked it out on a date?
A: I can see you, but only in a non-datal sort of way.

I didn't come here to be insulted. Where do you usually go?

Characters: Gin Bob Johanssen &Last Chance Sadie.

I'm not sick from life itself, it's just the ride.

Book Titles:
How to Have a Completely Bloody and Devastatingly Dangerous Halloween.
Can Morons Date?
We're Just Friends… Explanations and Justifications For Dating Ugly People.

What history left out about Robin and Marion after Richard returned from the Crusades.

Before Bathrooms.

**One day, while nursing a hangover, Picasso creates his
signature style.**

NAMES: Will U. Cowtip, Mary N. Ugliman, Senda Letterbom, Betty Ripserhoff, Imenna Paradox, Jess Fine N. Dandy, Russell Upsumgrub, R. U. Maninoff, Rusty Nail. Miss Possessive, Belle of Lugosi, Miss Interpret, Miss Haggadashery, Maleki Rooftop, Cartoon Asylum.

Where's the sanctity of singleness?

Adult Toys: Chubby Grinds: the dolls that gets a chubby when you rub its weinee, Liquefying crystal balls

Math terms: derivative, integral, and prerogative

I am not rectal, I always talk out my ass.

The bully: "Are you turning yellow?"
The coward: "No, my liver is just fine, thank you."

She's blessed with the counting of the ways.

You're so local.

I've been hit in the reality box.

I've been fishing for complements… you didn't have to cast too far.

I'm not a computer moron you know… the word idiot fits just as well.

Q: What did the transsexual exclaim when he was asked to make a cross-dresser film?
A: By gender, we'll do it.

Why cut your hair when nature will take it away from you anyway?

Milton didn't think that when the race started it would have helped him to remove the training weights from his ankles first.

Jonesy never fully recovered from that awful ordeal after the plane crash in the Himalayas.

I'm not going to sit in God's barber chair just yet.

I love it when you seethe.

I'll just sit here til I slither away from your empathy.

If flames came from a sense of humor you'd be an Olympic torch.

I can safely say that without any fear of contraception.

I'd rather be moron than more off.

Metaphor: You're cooking with lighter fluid now. I just need someone to supply the matches. Well they're out there. Maybe, but most of them are all wet.

Stress happens to the best of us when we have to endure the worst of them.

I need to find someone who is more geographically desirable. You mean like above ground?

Film idea: "Glass," the adventures of a piece of glass in metamorphic progression.

Aphorism: I should be paid for my life, not paying with it.

Cerebral Mixture: when you are proficient in different things with different hands but are not ambidextrous.

I live vicariously through anticipation.

Here I go, playing another round of destiny.

They can't be students, 'cause students are people who study.

I'm gonna rock your bones.

The monster is about to extenuate itself on us.

Welcome to fornication forest.

How did you get that? It was by propagation.

It is great talking with someone of quizzical intelligence.

Conversation at an intellectual café: "I'll have a retort with my latte, please."

Today I'll have dry heaves, tomorrow dry toast.

That's the problem with making your bed, you want to lie in it too.

You're so dorkus you're on dorkozine.

Don't dawdle in my skivvies.

You can't build up a vocabulary at the gym.

Film title: Well, At Least We Have Sunday.

Amusement park rides are like so many lives. They go around, but never get anywhere.

Silly Letter...

fr: 4567 Lost Suction Lane, Bristol, Tim Curry 00006757
Dear Silly Pants,
OK, so you have silly pants. When I was at Eton, I experienced
the fallout of being an upright vacuum cleaner, bloody hell it
was. I couldn't even get replacement bags that would fit my
upright frame. Anyway, I thought I'd razzle my thingwilley in
some expression of sand holster while spackling my tendernods.
So have a nice "who's your auntie" and stay shack in plastic.
     Sincerely and with pointed shellies,
     – Ms. Wilma Fatbottom Freestanding III

Well wank my grady.

They must be doing well, they're still rich.

Film title: *The Random Solution*

Everything is great in theory. It's much better in application.

Interactive PC's with built in "guilt" software.

The real reason George Washington fought in the Revolutionary War.

I told him someday he'd get laid.

Favorite Hollywood trends: Colonic cleaning—yummy! My favorite way to clean the old digestive tract. Nothing like sticking a vacuum up the old hole (either one). I'll stick to another trend, eating lettuce.

People in Hollywood are so star struck that all you have to do is look famous to inspire such comments as, "are you famous?", "Aren't you that guy from… ?", "I know you!", "You're you, aren't you?"

People in Hollywood also love to use big words that try to make themselves sound so impressive and intelligent. Words like laconic, which actually means concise, but to a local would be used in the following, "I feel so laconic today. I guess it's because I worked all night at the Gender Bender serving espresso." The sad thing is people in Hollywood might just believe it.

Did the chicken lay the egg? No, but it laid the hen.

Desperation breeds inspiration.

We are extraordinary without being arrogant.

Story idea: Johnny Wandering… about a man who sets off on a journey to spread happiness across the country in dire need of it.

Film Title: *Tangent of Evil.*

Name: Sandy Floors, Ethel Bargman.

Title: *Professor Stench Dracman's Rolodex of the Bizarre.*

CD-Absurdities
Song Titles: Lost in Frustration, Metagag, Don't put a Cow on my Salmon Spread, Outside the Crazies.

Excuse me, but by any chance, do you breast feed your baby?

The only clue he noticed led the detective to merely speculate on the real cause of death.

Like bacon through the pig.

Mellowtations.

Stay above debt and water.

I have a present for you. So, how many people have used it?

You can lead a horse to water, but a pencil must be lead (credited to Laurel and Hardy).

Don't stress for success.

I met my dream girl, but the sandman already gave her to someone else.

How was I to know?…
I ordered a Greek gyro platter that included yogurt. I asked if they had strawberry or banana yogurt. Everyone laughed. I never did get my yogurt and I've never been back to Greece.

In the last war I saved 500 men. How? I killed the cook.

TITLE: *The Thing That Couldn't Swim.*

How many hairs on the average human's head? Two! Why only two? 'Cause my uncle is average and he only has two.

I had a friend who coughed for twenty years. Tried everything, until he took this one bottle of cough syrup, and immediately stopped coughing. Why? He had a heart attack and died.

Do you believe in love at first sight? Sure do, the first time I saw a hamburger with all the fixin's.

EXPOSING PHONY HOLLYWOOD!

It was the only time he's even been "near" the truth.

Everybody in Los Angeles has an agent.

Names: scummy yummies, shaking jelly.

Egad: Darn your sox.

"Whatcha doing?" "I'm just sittin' around losing wait."

I'm not going to let people get me down. I will be happy no matter what. Just call me Johnny Smileseed.

Words to Love by: "All it takes is a hug."

I live for exposure. I can't live on it, but I can live for it.

I wouldn't pay him attention, much less pay him money.

Some people have drive. Nothing to offer, but they have drive.

Mr. Cold Shower: even his hand rejects him.

Silly Products: Schmeganstein, a small country known for their cheeseballs found at Falkenbergs cheese shops. They were created by Bathels and Jamus, who also were responsible for the first wine and cheese soirees.

Everyone is one dent short of botchalism.

There's nothing better than to have someone proud of you.

Encouragement: Go for the dream. There'll be people who try to hurt you and discourage you but don't ever believe it. For people put down what they can't have, your talent, your gifts, your love.

Last night, I laid awake dreaming and saw a nightmare in my head.

Names:
Psychedelinuts: cool people with outrageously creative minds.

Blabberate: To talk without thinking. (Synonym- Splurrgle).

I wasn't always a domestic goddess. I used to do this in Europe.

I used to wonder why my kids have no resemblance to me 'til I
saw what my wife looked like: then I was glad.

Baby Detective: I solved the mysterious diaper rash killings.
It was a smelly job, but I couldn't let innocent babies take the
dump for the real criminals.

You're undressing my hair with your eyes, aren't you?

I'll bet there's all sorts of panimlee animlies in there.

What makes Boston crème? Was it Cherrie's pie?

What's a scary thought like you doing in a concept like this.

If you snooze, you lose…if you never sleep you die. Get some
rest sometimes stupid.

Show Title: Fringe Celebrity: my life on spec.

Biceptual: possessing more than one concept (or for the more
banal… needing two bicepts to construct one thought).

Driblets: little creatures with no control over their glands.

My lips are dry. Do they look really weird? Only when you
talk.

How to kill that "first" date.

John of "Dear John" letter fame.

"Better be careful farmer Brown, there's polyester in there and she's got a cotton pickin' problem."
"I'll iron it out but it's a synthetic this had to happen."

Gabulating Nonsense: jibberish, useless spewing of unimportant tripe from the masticating region of the face.

You ran out of toilet paper in the bathroom so I had to use antiseptic wipes. Oh my gosh, don't you know, I have heavy dosages of recyclinated bathroom tissues in various pastel prints.

I have become a diluted alcoholic by putting soda in my wine.

Lost in cyberoblivion.

Observation: I saw a sign in front of a home construction site one day while jogging.
The sign read Kavin Construction. Now I don't know about you, but I would question having a man named Kavin handling such a punctilious task as building a stable house for me.

Character: Sherri Heath.
Observation: In LA, sometimes I feel like I'm swimming in a cesspool of vermin and I'm the only one wearing a bathing suit.

Song lyric: Digging to China why do fools fall.

Movie title: "The Thing From Over There."

Musical forms: "Bubblepunk," "Psychedelibubblepop."

One day a man got his penis chopped off. Upon noticing, his friend observed, "That's not a vasectomy, that's a di-sectomy".

When smart people say stupid things they let their intelligence down.

Everyone can have a forced occurrence.

You're a girl with muffins in your hair.

I can't make love to you unless you stay the night.
What does that have to do with making love?
It's called the Cuddle Factor.

I'm gonna get you Compound W to get rid of your worry warts.

I'm so past the point of over it.

He's just like Dustin Hoffman, just in a Caucasian way.

Where are the sox? They're by everything else. But there is a lot of everything else.

Little Scatternesses.

I'm unique, not a Eunich.

Did you take preventinations against that?

You can lose your love handles but leave the love.

I just don't freak out over one thing…I'm an equal opportunity freakist.

The annual philosopher/psychologist mixer.

Time's fun when you're having flies.

Q: Where do Jewish parents work?
A: At a guilt complex.

Sleep is the only thing people can lose without actually looking for it.

You choked on your own blame.

If you consider living off the street luxury, then yeah, these are luxury apts.

Some people can be a complete tool yet have no ability to fix anything.

I have a cast iron stomach but it's coated with Teflon.

Stew doesn't taste very good in a pity pot.

You don't like my nose? What's snot to love about my nose?

It's not contagious, like the flu, or death.

I have a photographic memory. I lost the prints, but at least I still have the negatives.

VIRGIL DIDN'T HAVE A FIRM GRASP OF HIS SURROUNDINGS.

New Board Game:
Save the Rabbi©
Objective: Save the Rabbi before he becomes Gentile. You must travel around the Temple to reach Mazeltov and save the Rabbi. Included: Game board, dreidel spinner, player pieces (Schlomo the Baker, Moisha the Yenta, Harry the Moil and Bernie the Accountant), yarmulkes.

Game board squares include:
> sitting shivah (lose turn)
> guilt tripped (go back two spaces in shame)
> You become a man (advance two spaces)
> Oye Vey (pick a card)

Cards:
> stump the Amish (ask a player to do a stunt and if they fail you can switch places with them if they are ahead of you)
> ask the Rabbi (in a Jewish accent, ask another player for forgiveness)
> the hit list (sing a song by a Jewish singer)

New cable network: The Amoeba Channel for single cell programming.

Dilemnic reality.

Band name: Phantom Residue

I would rather live in a happy delusion than a harsh reality.

Everything was healthy up to the register.

Once upon a time most recently, there lived a bear. A really extraordinary bear. Extraordinary because he cared.

An intellectual is someone who knows nothing and gets people to think they know even less.

Funourishment: Fun foods (like muffins or chocolate) that are good for you.

Let's just run away to success together.

For those who've ever taken a city bus…I would rather drag my zombie eaten carcass across the glass shard ground than to take a city bus.

Death is just a transition to Los Angeles.

Zombie: "I've lost my head many times, but never my temper."

Cynicism is our defense against false sincerity.

Man, when I'm dead and compost, maybe then someone will dig me.

From the overweight dept: I'm in such great shape, I am breathing…hardly.

When you help a crazy person, ask yourself who the real crazy person is.

Don't be a stranger. Just be strange.

❏

About the Author

Dave Shelton is a prolific and award winning film and television writer and cartoonist living in Los Angeles, California, with his fiance, Tami Zorge. He has worked for Nickelodeon, MTV, Disney, Klasky Csupo and Warner Bros. and with such stars as Tim Allen and Prince. He was head of cartoon projects and a senior writer at *National Lampoon* and rock journalist and cartoonist for *Tiger Beat* and *Rockbill* magazines. His work has also appeared in *16 Magazine, Star, WOW* and *Woman's World Magazine*. Dave is also the creator of the popular "Hackidu" characters from *Everybody Loves Raymond*. He has illustrated several successful children's books, including *The Lemming Shepherds*, and is the creator of the kids TV shows *Snuggy Bear and the T-Shirt Kids©,* and *Professor Creepy's Scream Party©*.